We Shall Overcome

A Song That Changed the World

BY STUART STOTTS

FOREWORD BY

Pete Seeger

WITH ILLUSTRATIONS BY Terrance Cummings

CLARION BOOKS | HOUGHTON MIFFLIN HARCOURT | BOSTON • NEW YORK | 2010

Clarion Books
215 Park Avenue South
New York, New York 10003
Text copyright © 2010 by Stuart Stotts
Illustrations copyright © 2010 by Terrance Cummings

The illustrations were executed in mixed media.
The text was set in 13-point Deepdene.
Book design by Sharismar Rodriguez

For information about permission to reproduce selections from this book, write to
Permissions, Houghton Mifflin Harcourt Publishing Company, 215 Park Avenue South, New York, New York 10003.

Clarion Books is an imprint of Houghton Mifflin Harcourt Publishing Company.

www.hmhbooks.com

Manufactured in China

Library of Congress Cataloging-in-Publication Data
Stotts, Stuart, 1957–
We shall overcome : a song that changed the world / by Stuart Stotts ; foreword by Pete Seeger ; with illustrations by Terrance Cummings.
p. cm.
ISBN 978-0-547-18210-0
1. We shall overcome—Juvenile literature. 2. Protest songs—United States—History and criticism—Juvenile literature.
3. Music—Political aspects—United States—History—Juvenile literature. I. Cummings, Terrance, ill. II. Title.

ML3561.W45S75 2009
782.42162'13—dc22

2009022578

LEO 10 9 8 7 6 5 4 3 2 1

For my father, Jack L. Stotts (1932–2008),
who never lost sight of the peaceable city

Contents

FOREWORD

No one can prove how important music is, but people in power believe it is, and they try to control it. Plato wrote that it was dangerous to allow the wrong kind of music in *The Republic*. There's an old Arab proverb: "When the king puts a poet on his payroll, he cuts off the tongue of the poet." In the USA, the powers that be have always tried to keep protest songs off the hit parade. But "We Shall Overcome" and other songs like it rose up anyway and helped to change the world.

The power of singing together shows us that change is possible. In Beacon, New York, where I live, adults and children gather every year for a big block party called "The Spirit of Beacon Day." There are people from different religions and different cultures speaking many different languages. There is singing, dancing, and eating. It is a hopeful event for everyone, and music helps to bring us together.

I've sung "We Shall Overcome" on all four continents. I've sung it with small groups and with a hundred thousand people. It's a confident song and a reassuring song. I see a mother singing it to her baby when there's bad news. I see groups of people singing it in times of trouble.

If the world is to survive, it will be because people everywhere learn to work together—in spite of our differences—to try to solve our problems. "We Shall Overcome" is a song that reminds us of where we want to go, and it helps us on our way there.

Pete Seeger

ONE

Keep Your Eyes on the Prize

We're gonna board that big Greyhound,

Carrying love from town to town.

Keep your eyes on the prize, hold on.

On May 20, 1961, twenty-year-old Bernard LaFayette Jr. stood with a small group of civil rights workers in a bus station in Montgomery, Alabama. An angry mob of segregationists surrounded the terminal. "Nigger lovers! Filthy communists! Go home. You're not going to integrate Montgomery!" they shouted at the white members of the group—the curses and threats they yelled at the black members are too vile to be repeated here. These angry men and women were intent on intimidating—maybe even killing—everyone who huddled in the station. Only a few federal marshals blocking the doors stood between the crowd outside and the group inside.

The civil rights workers were afraid, but they were determined to change society. In the 1950s, the federal government had passed laws declaring that there should be no discrimination on buses that crossed state lines. However, many southern states continued to insist that black and white passengers sit separately, with whites in the front of the bus and blacks in the back.

In the early 1960s, civil rights organizations decided to draw attention to segregation in the South. Bernard LaFayette was part of a small group of activists who were determined to integrate southern bus travel. They called themselves Freedom Riders. They boarded buses together, and the white riders deliberately sat in the back, while the black riders sat in front, challenging the federal government to uphold the laws. Mobs of segregationists often stopped the buses and beat the riders, and one man, a white minister named James Reeb, was killed.

Freedom Riders faced many serious threats. As this bus traveled through Alabama in spring, 1961, segregationists slashed its tires. After one tire blew out on the highway, a crowd blocked the bus door and trapped the passengers inside. Then someone threw a firebomb in through a window and the riders had to break through the emergency door. Seconds after they escaped, the bus exploded.

AP/World Wide Photos

Standing in the terminal that day, Bernard LaFayette thought of the times he had seen his friends threatened, attacked, and bloodied. He knew the danger he and the other Freedom Riders faced, and he knew how afraid they all were. But he also knew they had to find the strength to go on.

The riders joined hands in a circle and began to sing "We Shall Overcome." Many years later, Bernard recalled that moment. "The song has different meanings at different times," he said. "Sometimes you're singing about problems all over the world; sometimes you're singing about problems in the local community. But in that bus station, it was a prayer, a song of hope that we would survive, and that even if we in that group did not survive, then we as a people would overcome."

The mob stormed into the terminal. The federal marshals were powerless to stop them, and the Montgomery police stood by without intervening. The mob chased Bernard and his friends through the city. Bernard's ribs were cracked by punches. Another rider, John Lewis, was smashed over the head with a wooden crate. He lay bleeding in the street, ignored by the police. When the mob passed, he slowly made his way to the hospital, where several other riders also ended up that day. One of them, William Barbee, had been beaten so badly with a lead pipe that he would be partially paralyzed for the rest of his life.

Bernard LaFayette Jr. was a leader in the civil rights movement throughout the 1960s. This photo is from his arrest in Mississippi for participating in the Freedom Rides. Bernard went on to become a minister, an educator, a lecturer, and an authority on nonviolent social change.

Segregationists frequently harassed, beat, bombed, and even murdered Freedom Riders and other civil rights workers. This photo, taken on May 14, 1961, shows several Ku Klux Klansmen beating an African American man in the Birmingham, Alabama, Trailways Bus Station.

Although that particular day led to violence and severe injury, the Freedom Riders' work paid off. More activists came to support the movement. National newspapers and television networks covered the story. The whole country witnessed the violence of segregation, and many people responded with outrage, demanding that the government uphold the law. Soon afterward, the federal government committed more marshals and even the National Guard to enforce the integration of buses in the South.

Despite fear, pain, and injury, Bernard LaFayette and thousands of other civil rights workers like him persisted in the fight for equality. The song "We Shall Overcome" accompanied their struggle, giving them strength and hope to keep going. In the end, they changed America.

Once the federal government fully committed itself to bus integration in the South, National Guard troops were called in to protect buses from attack.

Police often arrested Freedom Riders for breaking state segregation laws. Once arrested, the prisoners were sometimes beaten or denied basic rights in jail. These men are singing to keep up their spirits as they are taken away in a police wagon.

We shall overcome,
We shall overcome,
We shall overcome someday,
Oh, deep in my heart I do believe
We shall overcome someday.

"We Shall Overcome" is not elaborate or complicated. The first verse has only twenty-two words, and most of them are repeated. The melody is straight-forward and easy to learn. The chords are basic. Overall, the song could hardly be simpler. Yet it has played a unique and important role in United States history. Even beyond our borders, it has provided strength, connection, courage, and faith to millions of people working to make our planet a more peaceful, just, and loving place.

TWO

Sing When the Spirit Says Sing

I'm gonna sing when the Spirit says sing.

I'm gonna sing when the Spirit says sing.

When the Spirit says sing, I'm gonna sing, oh Lord.

I'm gonna sing when the Spirit says sing.

WHO SANG THE FIRST SONG? When and where did we start singing? Maybe under a rock ledge or around a tree on an African plain or on an ocean beach, voices shifted from grunts or groans or clicks into what we would recognize now as singing.

Why did people sing? Did they want to imitate natural sounds? Did they raise a shared chorus to meet the full moon or falling rain? Did they sing for fun, or was there some deeper emotion of pain or triumph that brought out music?

Did these singers dance? Did they clap in rhythm? Did they pound out a beat with their hands on their knees, or on a log or a rock?

Archaeologists have found instruments that are thousands of years old, but there's no way to know when people first sang—although it was probably before they invented instruments. We can guess, however, that one reason people sang was to find strength together. In hunting, in planting, in battle, or in any other task that requires strength, singing helps. It coordinates breathing and focuses energy and effort.

War songs have accompanied people into battle for thousands of years. Similarly, work songs have helped people perform difficult tasks such as rowing, pulling, or hammering. The slaves who hauled huge stone blocks to build the Pyramids probably sang to find strength in the hot Egyptian sun, just as the slaves who toiled in the heat of the southern United States did thousands of years later.

This bone flute was discovered in a cave in Slovenia where Neanderthals lived more than 40,000 years ago. It was carved from the femur of a cave bear.
Courtesy of Jelle Atema

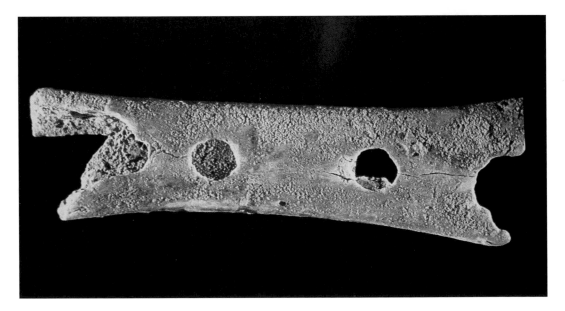

Enslaved people in the South planted cotton and tobacco. They hoed weeds. They harvested crops and carried heavy bales of hay to wagons and storehouses. They worked ten, twelve, even sixteen hours a day in the fields and homes of their masters. Sometimes they worked side by side with friends or family members, sometimes with people from different regions of Africa who did not share the same language or customs. Often they were whipped or beaten. Many resisted or fought back, but most lived without any real hope of relief or freedom.

This stereograph (an early form of photography) of women and children picking cotton in a field in South Carolina was taken in the 1870s, so the people pictured are not slaves. However, even after the Civil War was over, many freed African Americans continued to live and work for their former masters under very difficult, slavery-like conditions.

Photographs and Prints Division, Schomburg Center for Research in Black Culture, The New York Public Library, Astor, Lenox and Tilden Foundations

In the midst of suffering, they sang together. Some songs helped them work and find strength. Others helped them survive hard times, moving them to forget pain or weariness. And still others helped them believe in the possibility of freedom in this life or in the next. Some of these freedom songs later became the raw material for songs in the civil rights movement about a different kind of freedom.

In "Follow the Drinking Gourd," slaves passed the message to each other to follow the Big Dipper (the drinking gourd) north to freedom.

> *Follow the drinking gourd.*
> *Follow the drinking gourd.*
> *For the Old Man is waiting for to carry you to freedom.*
> *Follow the drinking gourd.*

In "Wade in the Water," which recalls the story of Moses and the Israelites' escape from Egypt, runaway slaves were advised how to avoid being tracked by bloodhounds.

Wade in the water.
Wade in the water, children.
Wade in the water.
God's gonna trouble the water.

The great writer and statesman Frederick Douglass described the music of the slaves this way: "[The songs] were tones, loud, long, and deep, breathing the prayer and complaint of souls boiling over with the bitterest anguish. Every tone a testimony against slavery and a prayer to God for delivery from chains."

Africans had their own music, brought from home, but they also learned Christian hymns from the religion of their masters. The songs they sang blended these Christian hymns with African choruses, rhythms, and phrases. Long after slavery ended, this musical mix continued in the South; and in the early twentieth century, the combination of African and European music laid the foundations for blues and jazz, as well as gospel music.

The early songs were constantly changing and evolving. Most enslaved Africans had no tradition of writing; they had always passed along history, stories, and songs by word of mouth. And very few were allowed to learn to read or write. Their masters felt that such learning would only encourage them to think for themselves and to be more rebellious. As a result, they could not write down words to songs, preserving the lyrics in one set form. When slaves were sold or traded to other locations, they carried the tunes and words in their memories. As a song spread, its melody, words, and phrasing changed. From one plantation to another, the same song was sung differently.

Frederick Douglass was born into slavery, and learned to read around the age of twelve. When he was twenty, he escaped by disguising himself as a freed black seaman and fleeing to the North. By the time this photograph was taken, in the mid-1800s, Douglass was one of the nation's most prominent abolitionists.
Library of Congress

On January 1, 1863, President Abraham Lincoln issued the Emancipation Proclamation, which freed by law around four million slaves in the South. However, it wasn't until the Civil War was over, in April 1865, that most of them were actually freed, and freedom in itself wasn't enough to guarantee a good life. Even after the war ended, prejudice and poverty made life very hard for former slaves. Songs remained important to them. Black church congregations sang the old work and freedom songs in their services, often changing the words to create religious meaning. These songs became known as spirituals, and they had a mixture of African and European influences. One of the songs, "I'll Be All Right," is similar in rhythm and structure to what we know today as "We Shall Overcome."

I'll be all right. I'll be all right.
I'll be all right someday.
Down in my heart, I do believe
I'll be all right someday.

Some scholars say that "I'll Be All Right" comes from an earlier slave song called "No More Auction Block for Me." However, "I'll Be All Right" was a religious song, and other verses included "I'll overcome," "I'll wear the crown," and "I'll be like Him," referring to following Jesus. Although the lyrics had a Christian focus, their intention of comforting and encouraging hadn't changed. Words of a song can offer a powerful message to a heart in distress. "I'll Be All Right" might be about the rewards of heaven, or it might be about relief from suffering and hope for a better life right here on earth. Either way, the message was compelling. The song became part of the river of words that flowed together to become the chorus of "We Shall Overcome."

Another source was a hymn by a man named Charles Tindley. Tindley was born in Berlin, Maryland, in the early 1850s. He had a hard life and little

This wood engraving shows a family being sold at slave auction in Virginia in 1861. Often, the members of a family were split up and sold to different bidders, and parents, children, and spouses never saw one another again. Photographs and Prints Division, Schomburg Center for Research in Black Culture, The New York Public Library, Astor, Lenox and Tilden Foundations

education. Although he was born free, when he was young he was rented out as a laborer. Charles later remembered: "The people with whom I lived were not all good. Some of them were very cruel to me. I was not permitted to have a book or go to church. I used to find bits of newspaper on the roadside and put them [under my shirt], for I had no pockets, in order to study the ABCs from them. During the day I would gather pine knots [pieces of wood], and when the people were asleep at night, I would light these pine knots, and, lying flat on my stomach to prevent being seen by anyone who might still be about, would, with fire-coals, mark all the words I could make out on these bits of newspaper. I continued in this way, and without any teacher, until I could read the Bible without stopping to spell the words."

Charles Tindley eventually became pastor of a church in Philadelphia. His eloquence and righteous dedication filled the sanctuary every Sunday, along with more than three thousand worshipers. They came to hear his inspiring sermons, to pray, and to sing. Besides being a great preacher, Charles wrote hymns that became popular in black churches throughout the country. Like his sermons, these hymns encouraged his parishioners to persevere in the face of poverty and prejudice. In 1903, he wrote a hymn called "I'll Overcome Some Day." One verse went like this:

This world is one great battlefield, with forces all arrayed.
If in my heart I do not yield, I'll overcome some day.
I'll overcome some day, I'll overcome some day;
If in my heart I do not yield, I'll overcome some day.

We don't know if Charles was familiar with "I'll Be All Right" when he wrote "I'll Overcome Some Day." Although the words carry a meaning similar to those in "I'll Be All Right" and in what later became "We Shall Overcome," the melody, lyrics, and structure of his hymn are very different from both.

These songs were the raw material that formed "We Shall Overcome." But the musical process of improvisation would have to shape them first.

THREE

There's a Meeting Here Tonight

Get you ready, there's a meeting here tonight.
Come along, there's a meeting here tonight.
I know you by your daily walk.
There's a meeting here tonight.

IN THE CLASSICAL MUSIC TRADITION OF EUROPE, musicians follow notes printed on paper, performing pieces as the composers, such as Bach or Mozart, meant them to be played. Although individuals may put their own stamp on a piece through the expressiveness of their playing, they don't change the notes or tempo. Charles Tindley's "I'll Overcome Some Day" arose from this tradition. Tindley wrote the words and notes, and congregations sang the hymn in a fairly similar manner each time, probably accompanied by a piano or organ.

The song "I'll Be All Right" comes from the oral tradition, in which improvisation is key. Improvisation means changing notes and words and adding your own ideas to fit your mood or suit the situation. Music isn't written down, and no one keeps track of composers. A song might be sung fast in one place,

I'll Overcome Some Day

"Ye shall overcome if ye faint not."

Charles A. Tindley

Copyright, 1901, by Hall-Mack Co.

Though many African Americans were not accustomed to written music, congregations around the country learned and sang Charles Tindley's hymns from printed copies like this one. Although "I'll Overcome Some Day" began as a written piece of music, it also served as an inspiration for "We Shall Overcome."

Tindley Temple, Philadelphia

slowly in another. The words might change from week to week. The melody, too, may vary from place to place, although improvising musicians generally stay in the same key once the song has started. People don't hesitate to change songs to suit their needs; it is even expected. In improvising, there is no wrong or right, as long as the changes fit the spirit of the song and the moment in which it is sung.

During the 1800s, thousands of spiritual and gospel songs circulated through the South. They were typically sung in an improvisational style. The songs weren't for soloists; they sounded best when groups sang them. They were also usually sung a cappella (without instruments accompanying them) and often included handclaps or foot tapping.

In 1845, one traveler observed that the only permanent parts in these songs were the basic melody and the chorus. "The blacks themselves leave out old stanzas and introduce new ones at pleasure. Traveling through the South, you may, in passing from Virginia to Louisiana, hear the same tune a hundred times, but seldom the same words accompanying it."

Twenty-five years later, another visitor to the South wrote that the freed slaves would sing the words of one spiritual to several different tunes; or they would take a tune that pleased them and fit the words of several different songs to it. And in 1899, a writer named Jeannette Murphy reported that a former slave told her that "old heads" like him used to make up songs on the spur of the moment. "Notes is good enough for you people," he said, "but us likes a mixtery."

The writer Clifton Furness once described a prayer meeting where he saw the process at work. First, the preacher read from the Bible, repeating phrases about "God's lightnin' gonna strike!" Then the crowd began to moan and sway. A rhythm began, and a man in front of Furness suddenly shouted, "Get right, soldier! Get right with God!" Furness describes what happened next:

"Instantly the crowd took it up, molding a melody out of half-formed familiar phrases based upon a spiritual tune, hummed here and there among the crowd. A distinct melodic outline became more prominent, shaping itself around the central theme of the words 'Get right, soldier!'

"Scraps of other words and tunes were flung into the medley by individual singers . . . but the trend was carried on by a deep undercurrent stronger than any individual present, with a mass of improvised harmony and rhythms. . . . I felt as if some conscious plan or purpose were carrying us along, call it . . . communal composition, or what you will."

This wood engraving shows an African American camp meeting in the South. Camp meetings, also called revivals, were popular religious events in the 1800s. People gathered to express their faith and to convert others to Christianity. For African Americans, camp meetings provided a place to gather with friends and family, away from white society. Singing was central to the experience, and most of the songs were based on old spirituals. Since people often came from far away, these camp meetings helped to spread songs around the South.

Photographs and Prints Division, Schomburg Center for Research in Black Culture, The New York Public Library, Astor, Lenox and Tilden Foundations

Church for African Americans was typically emotional and exciting. Services might last for hours. As this late-nineteenth-century drawing of an African American church in Cincinnati, Ohio, shows, congregation members often sang enthusiastically, clapped along, and shouted out during sermons. Church could be a welcome relief from the pressures of everyday life, and the music sung there conveyed powerful messages about freedom, suffering, and perseverance. Photographs and Prints Division, Schomburg Center for Research in Black Culture, The New York Public Library, Astor, Lenox and Tilden Foundations

In the late 1800s, church became the center of social life for many black people in the South. It was a place where they could congregate freely, support one another, and sing together. "I'm Gonna Sit at the Welcome Table," "Keep Your Hand on the Plow," and "I'll Be All Right" were well suited to improvisational singing. But classic songs, such as Charles Tindley's "I'll Overcome Some Day," could also be changed. The version of "We Shall Overcome" that we know today grew out of this tradition. In the process, a new song was created, and as it moved beyond the southern black community, its message of "overcoming" took on new meaning.

FOUR

WHICH SIDE ARE YOU ON?

Come all of you good workers,
Good news to you I'll tell
Of how that good old union
Has come in here to dwell.
Which side are you on?
Which side are you on?

IN THE FIRST HALF OF THE TWENTIETH CENTURY, workers in many professions demanded new rights in their jobs. They formed unions to bargain with their employers for better pay, safer conditions, and shorter hours. Laborers in textile mills and car factories, coal miners, bus drivers, and railroad employees were among the many groups that organized to improve life for themselves and their communities.

Often they went on strike. All the employees would refuse to work. They formed picket lines, marching together in a kind of human fence in front of the workplace, carrying signs that explained their demands. They wanted the public to know what was happening. They also wanted to make it more difficult for the owners to bring in replacement workers, whom strikers called "scabs."

Until the strike was settled, the place of business—a factory or coal mine, for example—would be shut down. The owners couldn't make any money. Of course, the employees couldn't either.

Unions had a hard time keeping workers united. Some people decided that they couldn't afford to go without pay. They crossed the picket lines and went to work in spite of the strike. Others were frightened into staying on the job. Owners hired thugs to beat up strikers, intimidate them, and break their spirit. Strikes could last for months. Sometimes the union members would give up and go back to work without having won the changes they wanted.

Strikers sang together to keep their hopes up and to rally enthusiasm on the picket line and at union meetings. Some of the songs—such as "Which Side Are You On?"—were written out of their experiences in the labor movement. Others were adapted from old folk and spiritual songs. "I'll Overcome" was one of these. Sometime in the early 1900s, an unknown labor singer changed the lyric from "I'll overcome" to "we will overcome." The song was no longer about *one* person getting through trouble; it was about a group getting through trouble together.

Women were an important part of the labor movement. The factories that they worked in were often as dangerous and demanding as those where men worked. This photo shows women in New York City in 1910, striking for better conditions and higher pay.

Library of Congress

In February 1909, a coal miners' union in Alabama published a letter on the front page of the *United Mine Workers Journal*. The letter said, "Last year at a strike, we opened every meeting with a prayer and singing that good old song 'We Will Overcome.'" This is the first printed reference to the song being used outside of a church setting.

The Alabama union was one organization, but it had to have two chairmen, one black and one white. The black workers sat on one side of the room; the whites sat on the other. State laws wouldn't allow them to sit together. We don't know what melody the miners sang or what words they used, but we know that this song helped them with their strike, and that black and white workers sang it together.

In 1945, at the American Tobacco Company in Charleston, South Carolina, workers went on strike for higher pay and integration of the factory floor. They earned ten cents an hour and were asking for thirty cents. The company offered them fifteen. It took a lot of courage for them to stand up to their powerful employers. As they walked the picket line, they sang "We Will Overcome" to keep their spirits up. The melody was much closer to "I'll Be All Right" than it was to Tindley's hymn, but it also bore a resemblance to "O Sanctissima," a hymn sung in Latin.

At the strike site, a labor organizer named Delphine Brown sang the song fast and added the words "We will win our rights someday." Another striker, Lucille Simmons, sang it slowly, in what's known as long-meter style, with every word drawn out. When people saw her coming, they said, "Now Lucille is going to sing that song slower than anyone ever sang it before."

In the end, the workers settled for fifteen cents per hour and an improvement in their working conditions. Their song, "We Will Overcome," continued its journey.

In 1932, Don West and Myles Horton had created the Highlander Folk School near Monteagle, Tennessee, to help unions in the South. People attended workshops

Zilphia Horton sang at labor rallies and workshops throughout the country for many years. In this photo, she plays the accordion as she teaches a song to farmers at the Highlander Folk School. The participants are holding pieces of paper with the lyrics written on them.

for a week at a time. They learned about union elections, strike tactics, and recruiting of new members. The school had a serious purpose, but Don and Myles also knew the importance of music in bringing people together. Myles's wife, Zilphia, made sure that evenings at the school included square dances, fiddle tunes, and group singing. She was a walking library of old-time songs, and she also encouraged people to change the songs to fit the circumstances of their lives.

This photograph shows Pete Seeger (right) singing "We Shall Overcome" in Mississippi in 1963. In the 1960s, he traveled throughout the country, working and singing for civil rights. He was quick to incorporate others' changes and additions to the song and how it was performed, such as singing while holding hands with arms crossed.

Photo by Herbert Randall, courtesy of Mississippi Digital Library

In 1946, after the American Tobacco Company strike, some African American members of the Charleston union came to Highlander. They taught "We Will Overcome" to Zilphia, and she began to sing it at workshops. People who attended carried it back to their own labor strikes and union meetings.

That same year, Zilphia sang the song for a young man named Pete Seeger in New York. Pete had spent years learning and performing folk songs, which are traditional songs that have been passed down orally. He had traveled with the legendary folksinger Woody Guthrie, and he later became part of a very popular folk group called the Weavers. Although Pete sang some of his own songs solo, he was mainly interested in tunes, new or old, that people could sing together.

When Zilphia taught Pete "We Will Overcome," he altered it to suit his own style of singing. He sped it up and accompanied it on his five-string banjo.

Soon after that, the title changed, too. Pete, or possibly Septima Clark, a teacher at Highlander, changed the word "will" to "shall." No one remembers for certain who made the switch, but many people adopted it. "It sings better that way," said Pete, "because it has an 'ahh' sound, instead of an 'ihh' sound."

Around the same time, another folksinger named Joe Glazer learned "We Will Overcome" from a Highlander student. Joe worked for labor unions, and he sang the song at strikes and on picket lines. In his book *Labor's Troubadour*, published in 2001, Joe recalled, "I was teaching what later became the anthem of the civil rights movement to white textile workers all over the South. These workers were from small mill towns and were probably strict segregationists. . . . [To them] it was a union song, sung in a union hall. It had nothing to do with civil rights." In 1950, Joe included "We Will Overcome" on an album called *Eight New Songs for Labor*, which was the first recording of it.

Not all union activity happened at workplace meetings and on picket lines. Labor organizers tried to reach as many people as possible with their message about workers uniting to improve their lives. Here, Joe Glazer sings union songs at a dinner event.

Wisconsin Historical Society, WHi-65504

The songs and the singing traditions of southern churches would eventually become a rich resource for the civil rights movement to draw upon, but it was the labor movement that first brought these songs out of the sanctuary and into the world of social change. Pete Seeger, Joe Glazer, and a few others sang the song as they traveled around the country. Union members shared it, just as slaves had passed around earlier versions. But throughout the 1950s, only a small network of activists and organizers knew "We Shall Overcome," and it was just one of many labor and spiritual songs they sang.

FIVE

Woke Up This Morning with My Mind Stayed on Freedom

Woke up this morning with my mind stayed on freedom.

Woke up this morning with my mind stayed on freedom.

Woke up this morning with my mind stayed on freedom.

Hallelu, hallelu, hallelujah.

On Labor Day weekend, 1957, the Highlander Folk School celebrated its twenty-fifth anniversary. Since 1942, the staff members had welcomed black people to their workshops and had insisted on equality and respect between the races. In the 1950s, the focus at Highlander had shifted from labor rights to civil rights. Many civil rights workers, including Rosa Parks, had attended training sessions. She returned to Highlander for the celebration, and Dr. Martin Luther King Jr. and the Reverend Ralph Abernathy accompanied her.

The year 1957 was still early in the modern civil rights movement. Only two years before, Rosa Parks had sparked the Montgomery bus boycott by refusing to give up her seat to a white man. Dr. King had taken his first steps as a civil rights leader during the boycott. He and Ralph Abernathy and several other leaders had also recently founded the Southern Christian Leadership Conference (SCLC), an organization dedicated to nonviolent protest against discrimination.

At this anniversary event, Pete Seeger sang "We Shall Overcome." Dr. King had never heard the song before, but afterward, on the way to a speaking engagement in Louisville, he kept humming the tune. "'We Shall Overcome,'" he said to his driver. "That song really sticks with you, doesn't it?"

> We shall overcome,
> We shall overcome,
> We shall overcome some day,
> Oh, deep in my heart I do believe
> We shall overcome someday.

In 1957, Martin Luther King Jr. was the featured speaker at the Highlander Folk School's twenty-fifth anniversary. He had been active in civil rights for only two years, but had quickly achieved national prominence for his leadership. In his speech, he said, "I have long admired the noble purpose and creative work of this institution [Highlander]. . . . You have given the South some of its most responsible leaders in this great period of transition."
Wisconsin Historical Society, WHi-52822

Although the song's tune is simple, its melodic shape offers some clues as to why it is so memorable. The first two lines repeat a very basic musical phrase. In the third line, the melody rises, and the only rhyme in the song appears: "overcome" and "some." It occurs within the line, rather than at the ends of two different lines, as in most songs, and each of these rhymed words is held. The highest note of the song falls on the word "some," which emphasizes the rhyme. The second-highest note is on the word "deep," which emphasizes the power of faith embodied in the song. The word "believe" is also held, and singers can add harmony to the note easily, so the song becomes more powerful when people sing it together.

The same year as the Highlander anniversary, Guy Carawan, a young folksinger in Los Angeles, learned "We Shall Overcome" from another singer, Frank Hamilton. Frank, in turn, had learned it from Highlander fundraisers traveling in California in 1954. He added guitar chords to the song for richness and harmony, and he sang it slowly with a strong, steady rhythm to give it a more soulful feeling. "I wanted it to be more like gospel music," Frank said. He often sang the song at music parties, and that's where Guy Carawan first heard it. Guy then carried the song with him in *his* travels across the United States.

In 1959, Guy Carawan and his wife, Candie, visited Highlander. Zilphia Horton had died, and the school needed a music director. Although he hadn't come for that purpose, Guy stepped in and began to lead singing in the workshops. When he shared "We Shall Overcome" with groups, he sang it the way he had learned it from Frank Hamilton. The song, in a new version, had come full circle.

Some of the white people who lived near Highlander didn't like the place. They thought the staff members were Communists, and they didn't like to see black and white people working together. The police didn't like Highlander either. They raided it several times, supposedly looking for alcohol, which was illegal in the county.

This photo shows Guy Carawan (left) singing with James Bevel (center) and Bernard LaFayette (right) at the Highlander Folk School in 1960. Highlander was one of the few places in the South where black and white people could mingle freely. Like Pete Seeger, Guy Carawan helped spread "We Shall Overcome" and other civil rights songs around the country. Wisconsin Historical Society, WHi-65503

Enemies of integration attacked Martin Luther King Jr. and Highlander with this billboard, which showed a photograph taken at the twenty-fifth anniversary. At the time, Communists were assumed to be enemies of the United States. Even though Highlander was not a Communist institution, merely saying that it was could damage its reputation. AP/World Wide Photos

One day, the police showed up as a weekend workshop on desegregation had just finished. They cut the electricity and made the activists sit in darkness as they ransacked the house, pulling out drawers and scattering clothes on the floor. The staff and their guests sang together to keep up their morale. When they began "We Shall Overcome," a high school girl named Jamila Jones was the first to sing the verse, "We are not afraid. We are not afraid. We are not afraid today. Oh, deep in my heart, I do believe that we are not afraid today."

The song gave courage to the activists and unnerved the police. One of them said, "If you have to sing, do you have to sing so loud?" The activists immediately began to sing even louder. When the police left, everyone had experienced the power of the song to help in a dangerous time.

Guy Carawan continued to teach "We Shall Overcome" at Highlander workshops and to travel the country, leading sing-alongs for civil rights and labor events. Despite a tradition of adapting songs within the church, not everyone was happy to hear church songs sung outside it—and for a different purpose. Guy Carawan said, "Some people were offended at first; these were very personal songs about salvation. . . . But soon they realized that these were *their* songs, and they could change them to express what they wanted."

In February 1960, eighty people from all over the South gathered to discuss and learn about sit-ins, nonviolence, and boycotts at a Highlander civil rights workshop. As Guy Carawan recalled, "If we were sitting too long or all talked out, we'd sing." A few months later, on Easter weekend, he was in Raleigh, North Carolina, for the founding meeting of the Student Nonviolent Coordinating Committee (SNCC—pronounced "snick"). College students in the South created this group to fight segregation and discrimination. A few of the organizers had recently attended the workshop at Highlander, and they asked Guy to sing "We Shall Overcome."

Later at that same meeting, some of the participants spoke up. Guy tells the story this way: "Those young singers who knew a lot of a cappella styles, they said, 'Lay that guitar down, boy; we can do the song better.' And they . . . sang it a cappella with all those harmonies that had a way of rendering it, a style that some very powerful young singers got behind and spread."

Dr. Bernice Johnson Reagon is a scholar, activist, singer, and the founder of the a cappella group Sweet Honey in the Rock. She also tells a story of that day: "They started to sing this song, and everybody stood in the room, and then, without any instruction, people reached for each other. . . . They took their right hand and crossed it over their left, and then they had to move together. It's a funny thing about doing this. You have to move together from the end of the row toward the center, because if you don't, the person in the center of the row will be destroyed. And you know sometimes, when you are fighting for freedom, you need some outside help, which is why the [SNCC activists] come to town, to tell you that you have to move together."

The students' commitment and the power of the song filled the room. Guy Carawan recalled the feeling: "They just heard that song and knew it was theirs—it expressed exactly what they felt."

From that moment on, "We Shall Overcome" became the anthem of the civil rights movement. People sang it at sit-ins, demonstrations, and marches. They sang it as they were being dragged away by police, and they sang it in jail. They sang it at churches, in meetings, and on picket lines. They sang it on buses, at lunch counters, and on the steps of county courthouses. They sang it holding hands.

"We Shall Overcome" spread throughout the South and throughout the country, until everyone on both sides of the civil rights struggle knew it—and knew what it stood for.

Once "We Shall Overcome" became the anthem of the civil rights movement, meetings and rallies across the country often ended in a spirit of unity, with everyone singing together and holding hands with their arms crossed. Photo by Herbert Randall, courtesy of Mississippi Digital Archives

SIX

The Welcome Table

I'm gonna sit at the welcome table.

I'm gonna sit at the welcome table

One of these days, hallelujah.

I'm gonna sit at the welcome table.

I'm gonna sit at the welcome table one of these days.

THE CIVIL RIGHTS MOVEMENT FOLLOWED A LONG TRADITION of using music to build spirit, strength, and determination. In the 1930s, John L. Lewis, a labor leader in the United States, wrote, "A singing army is a winning army, and a singing labor movement cannot be defeated. . . . When hundreds of men and women in a labor union sing together, their individual longing for dignity and freedom are bound into an irrepressible force." This tradition was never more powerful than in the 1950s and 1960s.

Some of the songs of the civil rights movement—such as "Oh, Freedom," "Ain't Gonna Let Nobody Turn Me Around," "Woke Up This Morning with My Mind Stayed on Freedom," and "If You Miss Me at the Back of the Bus"— were popular before "We Shall Overcome." During the Montgomery bus boycott in 1955, black people walked or rode in carpools and refused to take the buses. Coretta Scott King, wife of Martin Luther King, remembered that the meetings during the boycott "were attended by the maids and cooks, and janitors, and people who really used the buses a lot. And they would be there singing and praying for hours, sometimes, before the program actually started." These meetings frequently included hymns or adapted versions of old folk or spiritual songs. However, after 1960, "We Shall Overcome" became the song most associated with the movement.

People often added verses. Pete Seeger added "We'll walk hand in hand" and "The whole wide world around." Many other verses surfaced, including "We shall stand together," "We shall live in peace," "The Lord will see us through," "We shall be like Him," and "The truth shall make us free."

The Student Nonviolent Coordinating Committee (SNCC) Freedom Singers performed at a rally in Harlem, New York, in March 1965. Music touched audiences in a way that mere speeches could not.

Photo by Diana Davies, courtesy of the Ralph Rinzler Folklife Archives and Collections, Smithsonian Institution

As the song spread, the way people performed it continued to change. In 1961, in Albany, Georgia, civil rights organizers sang it as part of their campaign for integration. Although the melody remained the same, people began to add harmony, trills, and rhythms that gave the song extra power. Rising "ohs" and phrases such as "I know that" and "my Lord" became part of the song. For example:

> *We shall overcome,*
> *I know that we shall overcome,*
> *Oh, Lordy, we shall overcome someday,*
> *Oh, oh, oh, deep in my heart I know that I do believe*
> *We shall overcome someday.*

Although the song was powerful to listen to, it was even more powerful to sing, especially when you were surrounded by the strong voices of people who knew suffering but had faith in victory.

Bernice Johnson Reagon was one of the activists in Albany at the time. She said, "When I opened my mouth and began to sing, there was a force and power within myself that I had never heard before. Somehow this music released a kind of power and required a level of concentrated energy I did not know I had."

Charles Sherrod, a founder of SNCC, felt something similar. "When we rose to sing 'We Shall Overcome,' nobody could imagine what kept the church on four corners. . . . I threw my head back, and I sang with my whole body."

Bernice added, "If you cannot sing a congregational song at full power, you cannot fight in any struggle. . . . [But] you don't sing a congregational song, you raise it."

"We Shall Overcome" played a role in many important events of the civil rights movement: the Freedom Rides in 1961, the March on Washington for Jobs and Freedom in 1963, Freedom Summer in 1964, and the Selma-to-Montgomery marches in 1965.

The March on Washington for Jobs and Freedom took place on August 28, 1963. In this photo, Martin Luther King Jr. and other activists walk toward the Lincoln Memorial. The march received a huge amount of national publicity; more than five hundred reporters and photographers documented the event and helped to bring civil rights issues to the nation's attention.

National Archives

Over 250,000 protesters came together in the nation's capital for the March on Washington. Joan Baez, a folksinger known for performing traditional songs, sang "We Shall Overcome," and Martin Luther King Jr. gave his "I Have a Dream" speech, advocating racial harmony, at the Lincoln Memorial.

Freedom Summer was organized by civil rights groups, including SNCC, SCLC, and the National Association for the Advancement of Colored People (NAACP). They aimed to increase voter registration among African Americans in Mississippi. The Selma-to-Montgomery marches in Alabama were also intended to draw attention to the ways in which black people were kept from registering and voting. As activists engaged in these protests, they knew that violence was always a possibility.

Willie Peacock, a civil rights worker, once faced a crowd of violent Ku Klux Klan members in Mississippi. The Klan was dedicated to preserving segregation of the races and denying black people equal rights. Willie reported, "We must have sung 'We Shall Overcome' for thirty minutes, and when we finished singing, there was no fear. It put you in touch with a larger self that couldn't be killed."

John Lewis joined the civil rights movement as a teenager, participated in the Freedom Rides, and later became a congressman from Georgia. His skull was fractured on a day in 1965 still known as Bloody Sunday, when police clubbed and tear-gassed Selma marchers who were demonstrating for equal voting rights. "It was one of the most powerful and at the same time sacred moments when we would sing 'We Shall Overcome,'" Lewis later said. "Especially if you have been beaten, arrested, and jailed, and thrown into a paddy wagon, thrown into some waiting area, and the group just stands there and sings together 'We Shall Overcome.' It gave you a sense of faith, a sense of strength, to continue to struggle, to continue to push on. And you would lose your sense of fear. You were prepared to march into hell's fire."

At one of the civil rights marches in Selma, Alabama, Pete Seeger heard a "shout" following "We Shall Overcome." Apparently, some activists felt that the word "someday" in the lyrics was too vague. So a leader would call, "What do we want?" and the crowd would respond "FREEDOM!" Then the leader would ask, "When do we want it?" and the crowd would shout, "NOW!"

Joan Baez, Bob Dylan, and many other folksingers performed "We Shall Overcome" at rallies and concerts. When Joan Baez sang it at the March on Washington for Jobs and Freedom, she became the singer most connected to the song in the public's eye.
National Archives

When a policeman shot civil rights activist Jimmie Lee Jackson after a demonstration in 1965, SNCC leaders organized a march in Alabama from Selma to Montgomery. As the six hundred marchers tried to cross Edmund Pettus Bridge in Selma, police stopped them with tear gas, clubs, and whips. Pictures of the savage violence shocked citizens around the country, and the day later became known as "Bloody Sunday." Two weeks later, thousands of people participated in this five-day march from Selma that successfully reached Montgomery.

Courtesy of Mississippi Department of Archives and History

Although these large events drew media attention, there were countless other, smaller actions involving thousands of people throughout the U.S. Activists all over the country sang "We Shall Overcome," and it connected them with others who shared the struggle.

Singing mattered, in good times and bad. Cordell Reagon, a civil rights worker and a founder of the Freedom Singers, understood how important it was. "There was music in everything we did," he said. "If you had a meeting or were just around

Civil rights workers across the country sang "We Shall Overcome" in their local struggles. Here, Father James Groppi, a prominent local leader in Milwaukee, Wisconsin, and other activists sing as they demonstrate for fair housing.

Wisconsin Historical Society, WHi-5295

the office, somebody would just come out with a song. Or if there were bad feelings, tension—anybody would open up with a line of a song, and somebody else would take it over, somebody else would add a verse, and by the end, everybody would be hugging each other. You can't have a movement without that."

Over time, segregation laws were repealed, and politicians passed other laws that promised equality and justice. On March 15, 1965, President Lyndon B. Johnson introduced the Voting Rights Act to Congress. The act eliminated barriers that kept African Americans (or Negroes, as they were respectfully called at the time) from voting. In his speech, he said, "It is the effort of American Negroes to secure for themselves the full blessings of American life. Their cause must be our cause, too. Because it's not just Negroes, but really it's all of us who must overcome the crippling legacy of bigotry and injustice. And we . . . shall . . . overcome."

Martin Luther King was listening to the speech. He had tears in his eyes as he heard the president of the United States quote those famous words. A moment of victory had arrived for all of America.

On August 6, 1965, Martin Luther King Jr. and other civil rights leaders were invited to the White House when President Johnson (lower left) signed the Voting Rights Act. The act prohibited states from denying the right to vote to anyone based on race or color. It specifically outlawed literacy tests given at the polls, which southern states often used to disqualify African American voters.

Photo by Yoichi R. Okamoto, courtesy of the Lyndon B. Johnson Library

SEVEN

Peace Like a River

I've got peace like a river.

I've got peace like a river.

I've got peace like a river in my soul.

JOE GLAZER WAS OFTEN ASKED WHY "We Shall Overcome" became the main song identified with the civil rights movement. He wrote, "No one knows why. Making a song into an anthem for a movement is a matter of mysterious chemistry. 'We Shall Overcome' had what it takes, and people made it their anthem without having a contest and without taking a vote."

Many different influences came together to form the unique and original song "We Shall Overcome." The need arose to copyright the song in order to preserve and protect its integrity for the future.

Pete Seeger's music publisher, TRO-Ludlow Music, Inc., first published "We Shall Overcome" in 1960, crediting Zilphia Horton, Frank Hamilton, Guy Carawan, and Pete as authors. At Pete's urging, the copyright credit was revised to acknowledge the inspiration of African American gospel singing, members of the Food and Tobacco Workers Union, and the southern civil rights movement.

All royalties earned from the song are donated to the We Shall Overcome Fund at the Highlander Research and Education Center. The Freedom Movement distributes the funds annually to worthy causes. In this way, the song helps the community that influenced it.

"We Shall Overcome" continued to play a vital role throughout the civil rights movement. Gradually, social justice improved, although racial discrimination and prejudice continue to this day. After Martin Luther King was assassinated in 1968, civil rights issues were not on the front pages of newspapers as often as before. Much of the nation's attention had turned toward the war in Vietnam.

Vietnam is a small country in Southeast Asia. It was once divided into North Vietnam and South Vietnam. When the two began to fight each other in the late 1950s, the United States took the side of a puppet government in South Vietnam and sent troops to help. In 1961, only a few hundred American soldiers were stationed there. By 1968, over 500,000 Americans were fighting in Vietnam, and an average of 1,200 were killed each month.

Many Americans felt that the war was wrong and that the U.S. should withdraw its troops from Vietnam. Many young men did not want to be forced by the government to join the military and fight. Mass protests spread across the country, particularly on college campuses. The antiwar movement grew, and, as in the civil rights movement, protesters were often involved in violent confrontations with police.

The antiwar movement included people who had worked for civil rights, and they knew the importance of singing during protests. "We Shall Overcome" was still a favorite, but in a new fight.

Vietnam War protesters used many of the same tactics that protesters in the civil rights movement used: sit-ins, boycotts, rallies, and nonviolent civil disobedience. Here, demonstrators at the Concord Naval Station in California are arrested and dragged away.

In the early 1960s, Joan Baez had sung "We Shall Overcome" at civil rights demonstrations and marches and also in performances. Her 1963 recording of the song was even in the *Billboard* "Top 100" for one week, which helped it spread beyond the movement. However, when she sang it at the Woodstock music festival in 1969, the purpose of the song had changed. Now it was about stopping the war in Vietnam.

Demonstrators often sang "We Shall Overcome" along with Vietnam-specific protest songs: John Lennon's "Give Peace a Chance" and Country Joe McDonald's "I-Feel-Like-I'm-Fixin'-to-Die Rag," with a chorus that begins "And it's one, two, three, what are we fighting for?" Most of the protesters did not have the background in improvisational and a cappella singing that African Americans did through their churches, but they sang for the same reasons: to find strength, unity, and hope in difficult situations.

Marjorie Swann was one of the founders of the New England Committee for Nonviolent Action. She remembers one of their antiwar protests. "In the fall of 1965, we planned a demonstration at Fort Devens [Massachusetts], where they trained troops going to Vietnam. We had a group of between seventy-five and a hundred people who lined the road outside the gate to the base, holding signs

This photo shows Joan Baez participating in a protest at a military recruitment center. Her husband, David Harris, was imprisoned for refusing to be inducted into the army. The draft, which forced young men to join the military, was a major focus for protesters. Joan Baez incorporated the song "We Shall Overcome" into her many appeals for peace until the war was over. AP/World Wide Photos

and distributing leaflets. . . . A large group of people [civilians] who worked at the base and other local inhabitants came to see our vigil, jeer at us, throw or tear up our leaflets, etc.

"This local crowd was getting noisier and more unruly. We consulted among ourselves and decided to do some singing. Much to our surprise, some of the folks sang with us. We did the Beatles' 'Yellow Submarine' and other popular songs. Then we joined hands and started 'We Shall Overcome.' A few of the onlookers joined hands with us and sang; some of the others sang along from the 'safety' of the sidelines. . . . I have never forgotten those few people at Fort Devens who joined us in singing 'We Shall Overcome,' some of them only moving their lips as they remained alongside the jeering crowd."

The song continued to bring people together. In May 1970, there was a rally in Washington, D.C. President Richard M. Nixon had just announced that the United States had begun bombing Cambodia, a country bordering Vietnam, and 80,000 people gathered before the Lincoln Memorial to protest. Charles Knower, a peace activist, remembered the scene. "There were speakers on the main stage, but no one was paying them much attention. All of us were angry about this new phase of the war, but we didn't know what to do. Small groups stood talking with each other. It all changed when Pete Seeger stepped up to the microphone. He began to sing 'We Shall Overcome,' and suddenly, the whole crowd came together. We sang and felt unified and strong."

"We Shall Overcome" was not as central to the peace movement as it had been to the civil rights movement. But by the time the Vietnam War ended, in January 1973, the song had reached far beyond its mostly southern roots. One generation had passed it on to the next, and it had found new life and new singers, with its promises of faith, victory, and a better world.

Vietnam War protesters and people who supported the war often demonstrated near each other. Most of these encounters sparked name-calling and chanting, and sometimes violence broke out between the two opposing sides. AP/World Wide Photos

These demonstrators came to Washington, D.C., in May 1970 to protest the war and the killing of students by the National Guard at Kent State University in Ohio one week earlier. Tensions were high, and there were many clashes between police and protesters. AP/World Wide Photos

EIGHT

I Got On My Travelin' Shoes

I got on my travelin' shoes.

I got on my travelin' shoes, oh Lord.

I got on my travelin' shoes.

FROM ITS ROOTS IN THE SOUTHERN UNITED STATES, "We Shall Overcome" spread around the world. In June 1963, Pete Seeger recorded the song live at Carnegie Hall in New York City. Soon after, he and his family began a ten-month world concert tour. The recording, called *We Shall Overcome: The Complete Carnegie Hall Concert,* was released by Columbia Records right after they left.

Pete performed in Australia, India, Tanzania, Kenya, Israel, and many other countries, and everywhere he went, he sang "We Shall Overcome." When he introduced it in Indonesia, he said, "Here is a song that has accomplished a revolution in our country. I hope it can in yours." After the concert, Indonesian political activists told him, "Here, we have military men planning to rule our country. Songs are not enough to stop them." There was respectful disagreement between them and Pete.

When Pete and his family reached Europe in early 1964, he was surprised to discover that audiences already knew the song. They had learned it from his new recording, and they sang it with him at his concerts.

That same year, Martin Luther King Jr. won the Nobel Peace Prize. His acceptance speech, given in Oslo, Norway, included these words: "I accept this award today with an abiding faith in America and an audacious faith in the future of mankind. . . . I refuse to accept the view that mankind is so tragically bound to the starless midnight of racism and war that the bright daybreak of peace and brotherhood can never become a reality. . . . I have the audacity to believe that people everywhere can have three meals a day for their bodies, education and culture for their minds, and dignity, equality, and freedom for their spirits. . . . I still believe that one day mankind will . . . be crowned triumphant over war and bloodshed. I still believe that we shall overcome."

When he returned from Europe after receiving the Nobel Peace Prize in 1964, Dr. Martin Luther King Jr. received the Medal of Honor of the City of New York from Mayor Robert Wagner. Vice President Hubert Humphrey, Governor Nelson Rockefeller of New York, and more than 10,000 citizens attended the ceremony in Manhattan that honored Dr. King.

Library of Congress

This Russian protester has the words "united we shall overcome" painted inside his megaphone. Political movements all over the world use the phrase to symbolize unity and hope for their cause. AP/World Wide Photos

Language and cultural differences did not prove to be barriers for "We Shall Overcome." All over the world, when people worked for equal rights, peace, and justice, the song became part of their struggle. Migrant farm workers in the United States sang it in Spanish when they went on strike in the late 1960s. They translated it as "Hemos de Triunfar."

Activists in South Africa sang it to protest against apartheid, a very strict system of segregating blacks and whites, enforced by law from 1948 to 1994. When U.S. Senator Robert Kennedy toured South Africa in 1966, he stood on the roof of his car and led crowds in singing the song. Years after apartheid ended, Nobel Peace Prize winner Archbishop Desmond Tutu of South Africa reflected on the song's role in that struggle. "'We Shall Overcome' is not about eliminating an enemy," he said. "It's about winning over a new friend."

In 1971, in India, during the Bangladesh War of Independence, the Calcutta Youth Choir recorded a translated version of the song. The title was "Ek Din

Surjyer Bhor," which means "One Day the Sun Will Rise." It became one of the best-selling Bengali records of all time.

"We Shall Overcome" has been sung in troubled places such as North Korea and Beirut. In 1989, Chinese students demanded greater freedom in their country. When they faced government tanks in Beijing's Tiananmen Square, some of them wore shirts that said "We Shall Overcome."

In 2007, a Kashmiri singer named Shameema turned the song into a hit. Kashmir is a region of the Himalayas controlled partly by India and partly by Pakistan. Thousands of people have been killed in the violent struggle over this territory. The lyrics of Shameema's music video urged people to stop the cycle of violence. She sang, "Vultures have gathered overhead. People have been crushed by oppression. Come, let us resolve this question. We shall overcome."

The video, which showed Shameema against a background of snowcapped mountains, was regularly telecast on local cable networks. As the Reuters news agency reported, "Many Kashmiris, weary of separatist violence, remain glued to their television sets when the region's leading singer bursts into the Kashmiri adaptation of the popular U.S. civil rights hymn 'We Shall Overcome.'"

The song spread so far and wide that Julian Bond, chair of the NAACP and a close associate of Dr. King's, joked, "I wouldn't be surprised if, when we colonize the moon, there aren't little green people who will join their antennae and sing 'We Shall Overcome.'"

Over the years people discovered that the song is not just for social movements but also for personal strength. When Bruce Springsteen contributed a recording of "We Shall Overcome" for a Pete Seeger tribute album in 1998, it was seen in a new way. Jim Musselman of Appleseed Records, which released the album, explained: "I started getting letters from parents whose children had leukemia, and they said they were singing Bruce's version of the song to [them]. It was a way they could say, 'We'll overcome this disease.'"

Jim also remembered that after September 11, 2001, when terrorists flew airplanes into the World Trade Center in New York City and the Pentagon in Washington, D.C., he got a call from NBC. "They wanted to do a video of the rescue workers, and they wanted to use Bruce's [recording of the] song. . . . [It] was played every single hour on the hour by NBC News, and it gave people a sense of hope and soothed them."

Many New Yorkers drew strength from the song that day. Classical pianist Karl Paulnack recalled, "The first organized activity that I saw in New York, that same day, was singing. People sang. People sang around firehouses, people sang 'We Shall Overcome.' . . . That was the beginning of a sense that life might go on."

"We Shall Overcome" continues to be present at important moments in history. In November 2008, Barack Obama was elected president of the United States, the first African American to reach this office. On the night of his election, he spoke to a quarter million people gathered in Grant Park in Chicago, and to countless others glued to radios and televisions throughout the world. As part of his victory speech, he told the story of Ann Nixon Cooper, a 106-year-old black woman who had voted that day in Atlanta. He cited some of the changes in the United States that she had seen in the course of her long life, including the civil rights movement. He said, "She was there for the buses in Montgomery, the hoses in Birmingham, a bridge in Selma, and a preacher from Atlanta who told a people that 'We Shall Overcome.' Yes we can."

After the terrorist attacks of September 11, 2001, the determination of the United States to rise above the tragedy was evident in many ways. This banner above a baseball dugout in Arlington, Texas, on September 18, 2001, expressed the sense of resolve and strength shared by citizens across the country at that time. AP/World Wide Photos

In 2007, the then presidential candidate Barack Obama joined Congressman John Lewis and many others in Selma, Alabama, to commemorate the Selma-to-Montgomery marches. Only forty-two years earlier, police had attacked marchers in Selma as they demonstrated for equal rights. The Selma-to-Montgomery route is now a National Historic Trail.
Courtesy of Byron Buck

"Yes we can," the huge crowd chanted in response. Another racial barrier had fallen in the United States, and the song "We Shall Overcome" was once again part of the legacy of change.

"We Shall Overcome" seems to tap in to our deepest emotions. The Reverend Wyatt T. Walker, an executive director of the SCLC, said, "I have heard it sung in great mass meetings with a thousand voices singing as one. I've heard a half dozen sing it softly behind the bars of the Hinds County prison in Mississippi. I've heard old women singing it on the way to work in Albany, Georgia. I've heard the students singing it as they were being dragged away to jail. It generates power that is indescribable."

Sarah Pirtle, a songwriter and peace activist, first heard the song as a child in the 1960s. "I learned it at age twelve," she said. "When we sang it, the world changed in that very minute. As we sang it strong with our eyes closed, we were singing that truth into being. Each word had power and insistence. We were telling each other that this world we can feel in our bones is coming to be."

Frank Hamilton said, "I used to think it was just a song and didn't really make any difference. But now, I think it's like a good piece of literature, which can change your life. And it doesn't belong to anyone now; it belongs to everyone."

From the first song ever sung to a tune written just yesterday, music sustains us in hard times and helps us celebrate good times. We sing for pleasure and for relief from pain. We sing when we are in—or out of—love. We sing to gather courage and to offer comfort.

"We Shall Overcome" is a song of power and faith. Millions of people around the world have sung it as they reached out to others, and deep inside themselves, finding strength to triumph over trouble and hardship. We can trust that people will continue to find power in "We Shall Overcome" and other songs like it as long as we keep working to create a better world.

Author's Note

In 1963, the civil rights movement was gathering great momentum. Nearly every day brought more news of protests, arrests, and violence from around the country, especially in the South.

In August of that year, my father, Jack Stotts, had been a professor at McCormick Presbyterian Seminary in Chicago for only three days when the president of the seminary called him into his office.

"Jack, I want you to go on a trip for us," he said. "One of our students, a young Negro man, has been doing summer work with a church in Wilmington, North Carolina. Yesterday, he was arrested for leading his youth group in a song on the county courthouse steps. He's in jail, which has created a big uproar there. People from seminaries around the country are gathering with local civil rights groups to protest his arrest. It sounds like a dangerous situation. We want to show our support, and Jack, I'd like you to go."

"I'd be glad to go," my father said nervously. He had been active in the civil rights movement for several years. He knew how risky these situations could be. The possibility of beatings, intimidation, and even murder was never far away at civil rights demonstrations in the South.

"Excellent," said the president.

"By the way," my father said, "what was the song?"

"'We Shall Overcome,'" the president replied.

The following day, my father flew to North Carolina, arriving late at night. Early the next morning he went to the offices of the local civil rights organization. People there welcomed him warmly and told him they would like him to be one of four speakers at a rally later that morning. After the rally, they wanted him to participate in an attempt to integrate local restaurants. At that time in North Carolina—and throughout the South—there were laws prohibiting blacks and whites from eating in the same restaurants. The activists wanted to test these local laws and draw attention to this injustice.

My father quickly put together a speech and participated in the rally with other speakers. In his talk, he drew connections to the Bible and what it says about freedom and justice. The student who had been arrested had been bailed out of jail, and he spoke as well. There was singing, too. My father, who was never very musical, felt embarrassed because he had a hard time clapping in time to the music.

Civil rights activists often focused integration attempts on restaurants and lunch counters. In this photograph taken in Atlanta, Georgia, in 1963, two people are picketing against the segregation policies of a restaurant. The African American protester's sign reads: I CAN COOK THE FOOD, BUT I CAN'T EAT IT.

Library of Congress

Afterward, he went off to a restaurant with one other white man and two black men. Several other racially mixed teams went to different restaurants around the city. The organizers hoped that the police would arrest each team for breaking the segregation laws, and the jail would be filled with protesters. My father's entire group felt frightened as they headed out together. They all knew how similar situations had often turned violent.

They went to their assigned restaurant, sat down together at a table, and waited. Nothing happened. The waitresses ignored them when they tried to order. The other customers gave them dirty looks and made comments under their breath, but no one confronted them directly.

From the beginning, the plan had been to wait for four hours. After that time, and after not being served or arrested, the team left without incident. My father was relieved. He was willing to go to jail for what he believed, but he was also glad he didn't have to.

Late in the afternoon, all the groups and organizers gathered again at the courthouse for more speeches and songs. No one had been arrested in any of the restaurants. The authorities probably wanted to avoid confrontations that would increase the tension in the city. That night, my father flew home. He was glad that there had been no violence or further arrests, but he also felt even more committed to civil rights.

My father continued to work for social justice throughout his life. I remember going with him to rallies and churches, where we often joined in singing "We Shall Overcome."

I have been a musician for many years. A while ago, I was asked to sing "We Shall Overcome" at a memorial service for a community leader. I hit the first chord on my guitar and began to sing. However, the crowd had a different tempo and feeling in mind. The song took on a rhythm of its own, and I stepped back from the microphone as the internal pulse of the crowd carried the words far beyond where I could have taken them.

On October 2, 2007, students from the Philosophy Day School in New York City sang in front of the statue of Mahatma Gandhi to celebrate his birthday. The United Nations General Assembly declared that date the International Day of Nonviolence, and students acknowledged the power of nonviolence to make change by singing "We Shall Overcome." AP/World Wide Photos

"We Shall Overcome" truly has a life of its own. I believe that learning about the song can help us to understand the civil rights movement—as well as other struggles for peace and justice—in our country's history. Many people placed themselves at great risk for the ideals of equality and fair treatment. Songs, especially "We Shall Overcome," helped them to find strength in their struggle for a better world.

We Shall Overcome

Musical and Lyrical adaptation by
ZILPHIA HORTON, FRANK HAMILTON,
GUY CARAWAN and PETE SEEGER.
Inspired by African American Gospel Singing,
members of the Food & Tobacco Workers Union, Charleston, SC,
and the southern Civil Rights Movement.

Moderately slow with determination (♩ = 66)

1. We shall o - ver - come,_____ We shall o - ver - come,_____
2. We'll walk hand in hand,_____ We'll walk hand in hand,_____

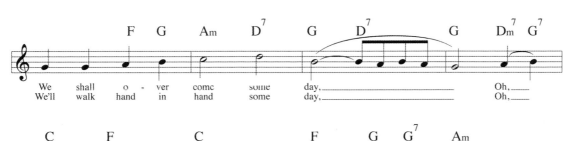

We shall o - ver come some day,_____ Oh,____
We'll walk hand in hand some day,_____ Oh,____

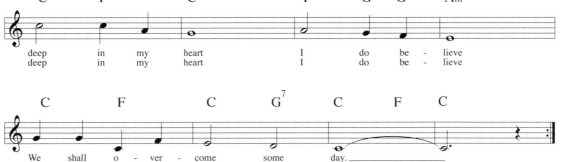

deep in my heart I do be - lieve
deep in my heart I do be - lieve

We shall o - ver - come some day._____
We shall o - ver - come some day._____

3. We are not afraid, we are not afraid,
   We are not afraid today,
   Oh, deep in my heart I do believe
   We shall overcome some day.

4. We shall stand together, we shall stand together,
   We shall stand together—now,
   Oh, deep in my heart I do believe
   We shall overcome some day.

5. The truth will make us free, the truth will make us free,
   The truth will make us free some day,
   Oh, deep in my heart I do believe
   We shall overcome some day.

6. The Lord will see us through, the Lord will see us through,
   The Lord will see us through some day,
   Oh, deep in my heart I do believe
   We shall overcome some day.

7. We shall live in peace, we shall live in peace,
   We shall live in peace some day,
   Oh, deep in my heart I do believe
   We shall overcome some day.

8. The whole wide world around, the whole wide world around,
   The whole wide world around some day,
   Oh, deep in my heart I do believe
   We shall overcome some day.

9. We shall overcome, we shall overcome,
   We shall overcome some day,
   Oh, deep in my heart I do believe
   We shall overcome some day.

Source Notes

These notes offer information about sources for each chapter. Unless otherwise indicated, references are to works cited in the bibliography. The works are cited by the author's name.

ONE Keep Your Eyes on the Prize

Chapter opening lyrics: Carawan and Carawan, p. 111

Bernard LaFayette and the Freedom Riders: Seeger and Reiser, pp. 52–58

TWO Sing When the Spirit Says Sing

Chapter opening lyrics: Gemini, *Good Mischief* (recording)

Ancient flutes: http://whyfiles.org/114music/4.html

Songs of the slaves: Douglass, p. 65

Roots of "I'll Be All Right": Author interview with Pete Seeger, 2005

Charles Tindley and his church: Tindley, p. 3

THREE There's a Meeting Here Tonight

Chapter opening lyrics: Various artists, *We Shall Overcome* (recording)

Melody and chorus as permanent parts of songs: Levine, p. 29

Fitting new words into old songs: Chase, p. 243

Former slaves making up new songs: Jackson, p. 328

Prayer meeting improvisation: Furness, p. 49

FOUR Which Side Are You On?

Chapter opening lyrics: Seeger and Reiser, pp. 64–65

Black and white union members singing together: Letwin, pp. 151–52, 256

American Tobacco Workers strike: Seeger and Reiser, pp. 8–9, and author interview with Pete Seeger, 2005

Highlander Folk School history: Seeger and Reiser, pp. 3–7, and author interview with Pete Seeger, 2005

"We Shall Overcome" as labor song: Glazer, p. 34

FIVE Woke Up This Morning with My Mind Stayed on Freedom

Chapter opening lyrics: Carawan and Carawan, pp. 83–85

Highlander anniversary: Author interview with Pete Seeger, 2005

Martin Luther King comment on song: Author interview with Pete Seeger, 2005, 2007

Learning and changing the song in California: Author interview with Frank Hamilton, 2008, and with Guy and Candie Carawan, 2007

Highlander police raid and new verse: Author interview with Guy Carawan, 2001, 2007

SNCC first meeting: Author interview with Guy Carawan, 2007, and Bernice Johnson Reagon
    quoted in *Sweet Honey in the Rock: Singing for Freedom* video

SIX THE WELCOME TABLE

Chapter opening lyrics: Carawan and Carawan, p. 18

Singing army: John L. Lewis quoted in Thomas, p. 41

Meetings during the bus boycott: Coretta Scott King quoted in *Eyes on the Prize* video

Changes to song in Albany, Georgia: *We Shall Overcome* video

Singing with power: Bernice Johnson Reagon quoted in Carson, p. 59

Singing with the whole body: Charles Sherrod quoted in Chafe, p. 163

Raising a song: Bernice Johnson Reagon quoted in Greenberg, p. 113

Singing when facing the Ku Klux Klan: Willie Peacock quoted in *We Shall Overcome* video

Power of "We Shall Overcome": John Lewis quoted on *All Things Considered*, NPR, January 15, 1999

Shout following song: Author interview with Pete Seeger, 2006

Singing around the office: Cordell Reagon quoted in Seeger and Reiser, p. 85

Voting Rights Act: Lyndon Johnson speech, Torricelli, p. 262

Martin Luther King watching speech: John Lewis interview, MSNBC, November 4, 2008

SEVEN PEACE LIKE A RIVER

Chapter opening lyrics: The Jordanairs, *Believe* (recording)

"We Shall Overcome" as anthem: Glazer, p. 35

Song copyright: Author interview with Pete Seeger, 2007

Singing at Fort Devens: Author interview with Marjorie Swann, 2008

Vietnam protest in Washington, D.C.: Author interview with Charles Knower, 2008

EIGHT I GOT ON MY TRAVELIN' SHOES

Chapter opening lyrics: Carawan and Carawan, pp. 118–19

Pete Seeger traveling: Author interview with Pete Seeger, 2005

Nobel Peace Prize acceptance speech: King, p. 107

Winning friends through song: Archbishop Desmond Tutu quoted in *We Shall Overcome* video

Kashmir version: Reuters News Agency, February 2007

Little green men: Julian Bond quoted in *We Shall Overcome* video

Personal importance of song: Jim Musselman interviewed in *Democracy Now*, 2004

Singing in response to 9/11: Karl Paulnack, speech to incoming freshman, Boston Conservatory of
    Music, September 4, 2004

Barack Obama's election night speech: *New York Times*, November 5, 2008

Tapping into deepest emotions: Wyatt T. Walker quoted in *We Shall Overcome* video

Learning the song as a young girl: Author interview with Sarah Pirtle, 2008

Importance of "We Shall Overcome": Author interview with Frank Hamilton, 2008

Bibliography

Books for Younger Readers

Bausum, Ann. *Freedom Riders: John Lewis and Jim Zwerg on the Front Lines of the Civil Rights Movement.* Washington, D.C.: National Geographic, 2006.

Bullard, Sara. *Free At Last: A History of the Civil Rights Movement and Those Who Died in the Struggle.* New York: Oxford University Press, 1993.

Finlayson, Reggie. *We Shall Overcome: The History of the American Civil Rights Movement.* Minneapolis: Lerner, 2003.

McWhorter, Diane. *A Dream of Freedom: The Civil Rights Movement from 1954 to 1968.* New York: Scholastic, Inc., 2004.

Rappaport, Doreen, illus. by Shane W. Evans. *Free at Last!: Stories and Songs of Emancipation.* Cambridge, Mass.: Candlewick Press, 2004.

———. *No More!: Stories and Songs of Slave Resistance.* Cambridge, Mass.: Candlewick Press, 2002.

———. *Nobody Gonna Turn Me 'Round: Stories and Songs of the Civil Rights Movement.* Cambridge, Mass.: Candlewick Press, 2006.

Books and Periodicals for Older Readers

Boyd, Herb, with CDs narrated by Ossie Davis and Ruby Dee. *We Shall Overcome.* Naperville, Ill.: Sourcebooks, 2004.

Carawan, Guy, and Candie Carawan. *Sing for Freedom: The Story of the Civil Rights Movement Through Its Songs.* New York: Oak Publications, 1990.

Carson, Clayborne. *In Struggle: SNCC and the Black Awakening of the 1960s.* Cambridge, Mass.: Harvard University Press, 1995.

Chafe, William Henry. *The Unfinished Journey: America Since World War II.* New York: Oxford University Press, 2006.

Chase, Gilbert. *America's Music, from the Pilgrims to the Present,* 2nd ed. Champaign: University of Illinois Press, 1966.

Douglass, Frederick. *My Bondage and My Freedom.* Champaign: University of Illinois Press, 1987.

Dunaway, David King. *How Can I Keep from Singing?: The Ballad of Pete Seeger.* New York: Villard, 2008.

Eyerman, Ron, and Andrew Jamison. *Music and Social Movements: Mobilizing Traditions in the Twentieth Century.* New York: Cambridge University Press, 1998.

Fulop, Timothy Earl, and Albert J. Raboteau, eds. *African-American Religion: Interpretive Essays in History and Culture.* New York: Routledge, 1997.

Furness, Clifton. "Communal Music Among Arabians and Negroes," *Musical Quarterly,* vol. XVI, January 1930.

Glazer, Joe. *Labor's Troubadour.* Champaign: University of Illinois Press, 2001.

Greenberg, Cheryl Lynn. *Circle of Trust.* Rutgers, N.J.: Rutgers University Press, 1998.

Jackson, Bruce. *The Negro and His Folklore in Nineteenth-Century Periodicals.* Austin: American
    Folklore Society, 1967.

King, Dr. Martin Luther, Jr. *I Have a Dream: Writings and Speeches That Changed the World.* New York:
    HarperOne, 1992.

Letwin, Daniel. *The Challenge of Interracial Unionism: Alabama Coal Miners, 1878–1921.* Chapel Hill,
    N.C.: University of North Carolina Press, 1998.

Levine, Lawrence. *Black Culture and Black Consciousness: Afro-American Folk Thought from Slavery to Freedom.*
    New York: Oxford University Press, 1978.

Reagon, Bernice Johnson. *The Songs of the Civil Rights Movement: 1955–65, A Study in Culture History.*
    Dissertation, Howard University, 1975.

Reagon, Bernice Johnson, ed. *We'll Understand It Better By and By: Pioneering African American Gospel
    Composers.* Washington, D.C.: Smithsonian Institution Press, 1992.

Seeger, Pete. *Where Have All the Flowers Gone: A Musical Autobiography.* Bethlehem, Pa.: SingOut!
    Corporation, 1993.

Seeger, Pete, and Bob Reiser. *Everybody Says Freedom: A History of the Civil Rights Movement in Songs and
    Pictures.* New York: W. W. Norton, 1989.

Thomas, G. "Hear the Music Ringing." *Georgia State University Review,* Summer, 1968. Atlanta: Georgia
    State University.

Tindley, Charles A. *A Book of Sermons.* Philadelphia: Edward T. Duncan, 1910.

Torricelli, Robert, and Andrew Carroll, eds. *In Our Own Words: Extraordinary Speeches of the 20th Century.*
    New York: Washington Square Press, 2000.

Warren, Gwendolin Sims. *Ev'ry Time I Feel the Spirit: 101 Best-Loved Psalms, Gospel Hymns, and Spiritual Songs
    of the African-American Church.* New York: Henry Holt, 1997.

Williams, Juan. *Eyes on the Prize: American Civil Rights Years, 1954–1965.* New York: Penguin Books, 1988.

Zinn, Howard. *SNCC: The New Abolitionists.* Cambridge, Mass.: South End Press, 2002.

RECORDINGS

Baez, Joan. *Joan Baez in Concert,* Part 2. Vanguard Records, 1963.

Barchas, Sarah, and the De Colores Chorus. *Bridges Across the World: A Multicultural Songfest.* High
    Haven Music, 1999.

Gemini. *Good Mischief.* Gemini Records, 1982.

Harley, Bill. *I'm Gonna Let It Shine: A Gathering of Voices for Freedom.* Round River Records, 1990.

Harris, Kim and Reggie. *Get on Board!: Underground Railroad and Civil Rights Freedom Songs,* vol. 2.
    Appleseed Recordings, 2007.

Harris, Kim and Reggie, and Rabbi Jonathan Kligler. *Let My People Go: A Jewish and African American
    Celebration of Freedom.* Appleseed Recordings, 2005.

Jordaniars, The. *Believe: A Collection of Bluegrass Hymns.* Madacy Christian, 2005.

Seeger, Pete. *Pete Seeger: How Can I Keep from Singing? A Radio Documentary Series.* Dunaway Productions,
    2008.

———.*We Shall Overcome: The Complete Carnegie Hall Concert.* Columbia Records, 1963.

Sing for Freedom: The Story of the Civil Rights Movement Through Its Songs. Various Artists. Smithsonian
   Folkways, 1990.

Springsteen, Bruce. *We Shall Overcome: The Seeger Sessions.* Columbia Records, 2006.

Sweet Honey in the Rock. *All for Freedom.* Music for Little People, 1992.

———. *Sacred Ground.* Earthbeat Records, 1995.

———. *Sweet Honey in the Rock.* Flying Fish Records, 1976.

Voices of the Civil Rights Movement: Black American Freedom Songs 1960–1966. Various Artists. Smithsonian
   Folkways, 1997.

We Shall Overcome: Songs of the Freedom Riders and the Sit-Ins. Various Artists. Folkways Records, 1961.

Where Have All the Flowers Gone: The Songs of Pete Seeger. Various Artists. Appleseed Recordings, 1998.

FILMS, VIDEOS, DVDs

Eyes on the Prize. Blackside, Inc., 1986.

Freedom Song. Horner, James, and Sweet Honey in the Rock. Sony, 2000.

Pete Seeger: The Power of Song. Jim Brown Productions, 2007.

Sweet Honey in the Rock: Singing for Freedom. Music for Little People, 2005.

We Shall Overcome. Jim Brown, Ginger Brown, Harold Leventhal, and George Stoney, 1989.

WEBSITES

www.crmvet.org. A website by and for veterans of the southern freedom movement of the 1960s.

www.democracynow.org. Source of interviews with Pete Seeger and Jim Musselman.

www.highlandercenter.org. Information about the programs, goals, and history of the
   Highlander Center.

www.npr.org/templates/story/story.php?storyId=1031839 and

www.npr.org/templates/story/story.php?storyId=1031840. A two-part series on the history of
   "We Shall Overcome," originally broadcast on NPR's *All Things Considered,* January 15, 1999.

www.nps.gov/history/nr/travel/civilrights. Information about historic places of the civil
   rights movement.

www.pbs.org/wgbh/amex/eyesontheprize/about/fr.html. Information about the TV series
   Eyes on the Prize, with links to other websites about the civil rights movement.

http://peteseeger.net. A Pete Seeger appreciation website, with links to many other folk music sites.

www.peteseegermusic.com. A listing of Pete Seeger's recordings and a history of his relationship with
   Appleseed Records.

http://whyfiles.org/114music/4.html. An article about ancient instruments written by the Why Files staff.

AUTHOR INTERVIEWS

Guy Carawan, 2001 | Guy and Candie Carawan, 2007 | Frank Hamilton, 2008 | Charles Knower,
2008 | Sarah Pirtle, 2008 | Pete Seeger, 2005, 2006, 2007 | Marjorie Swann, 2008

Acknowledgments

Thanks to Pete Seeger, Peter Berryman, Guy and Candie Carawan, Len Chandler, Jerry Chernow, Barbara Chusid, Kate FitzGerald-Fleck, Richard Ely, Kim and Reggie Harris, Phil Hoose, Charles Knower, Dan Little, Bradley Lyttle, Maia McNamara, Bobbie and Bill Malone, John Nichols, Cerisa and Calli Obern, Debra Orenstein, Tom Pease, Sarah Pirtle, Margie Rosenkranz, Megan Schliesman, Sheri Sinykin, Sarah Sprague, Norm Stockwell, Judith Strasser, Marjorie Swann. Deep gratitude to Terrance Cummings for his exceptional artwork, and to Marcia Leonard and Lynne Polvino for their vision, encouragement, and careful attention. Special thanks to my family, especially my wife, Heather, for the music we make together.

INDEX

Note: Page numbers in **bold** type refer to illustrations and their captions.